the MiSADVeNTU

vol.
3

MiCHAEL McMiCHAELS

the CREEPY CAMPERS

DISCARD

by **Tony Penn**
illustrated by **Brian Martin**

BOYS TOWN Press

Boys Town, Nebraska

The Adventures of Michael McMichaels, Vol 3: The Creepy Campers
Text and Illustrations Copyright © 2017 by Father Flanagan's Boys' Home
978-1-944882-10-5

Published by the Boys Town Press
14100 Crawford St.
Boys Town, NE 68010

For a Boys Town Press catalog, call 1-800-282-6657
or visit our website: BoysTownPress.org

Publisher's Cataloging-in-Publication Data

Names: Penn, Tony, 1973-, author. | Martin, Brian (Brian Michael), 1978-
    illustrator.

Title: The misadventures of Michael McMichaels. Vol. 3 : the creepy campers / by
    Tony Penn ; illustrated by Brian Martin.

Description: Boys Town, NE : Boys Town Press, [2017] | Audience: grades 1-5. |
    Summary: Michael and his fellow campers are surrounded by spooky woods and
    doing all they can to win the camp competition. The taste of victory becomes so
    sweet for Michael he can't stop bending the rules...even as his guilty conscience
    grows heavy. Author Tony Penn's expertly-crafted plot and sharp dialogue help
    children see the many real consequences of cheating and deception.--Publisher.
    Identifiers: ISBN: 978-1-944882-10-5

Subjects: LCSH: Truthfulness and falsehood--Juvenile fiction. | Honesty--Juvenile
    fiction. | Attention-seeking--Juvenile fiction. | Peer pressure--Juvenile fiction.
    | Camping--Juvenile fiction. | Ghost stories. | Interpersonal communication
    in children--Juvenile fiction. | Interpersonal relations in children--Juvenile
    fiction. | Children--Life skills guides. | CYAC: Honesty--Fiction. | Attention-
    seeking--Fiction. | Peer pressure--Fiction. | Camping--Fiction. | Ghosts--Fiction.
    | Behavior--Fiction. | Interpersonal communication--Fiction. | Interpersonal
    relations--Fiction. | Conduct of life. | BISAC: JUVENILE FICTION / Humorous
    Stories. | JUVENILE FICTION / Readers / Chapter Books. | JUVENILE
    FICTION / Social Themes / Peer Pressure. | JUVENILE FICTION / Social
    Themes / Values & Virtues. | EDUCATION / Counseling / General.

Classification: LCC: PZ7.1.P456 M4723 2017 | DDC: [Fic]--dc23

Boys Town Press is the publishing division of
Boys Town, a national organization serving
children and families.

10 9 8 7 6 5 4 3 2 1

For Joe, Lisa, Sophia, Adrianna, and Joey

Day 1

MY LIFE STINKS!

It stinks worse than my dog on the day we finally decide to bathe him. We don't stick to a schedule, we just wait until he stinks and then my mother usually makes a face and tells me or my brother, Joey, to wash him.

What stinks about my life is my friend Kenny and I are at a really intense camp this week and I thought it would be relaxing, but it turned out to be really stressful from the moment we arrived. I didn't want to do anything during our week off from school, but Kenny asked if I would like to join him in New Mexico at a camp he ASSURED me would be fun. My parents said it sounded like a good idea, and so off we went! Kenny's parents took the flight with us down here and neither of them could answer my question about how much 'newer' this Mexico was than the country of Mexico, which they don't call 'Old' Mexico for some reason.

Anyway, the camp is in the middle of nowhere, even though I don't know where nowhere ends and have no real way of knowing whether or not it is exactly in the middle, but you get the point. When we arrived at the camp, Kenny's parents said a big dramatic good bye to us like we were never going to see them again. It was super embarrassing, I'll be honest.

Our "Intake Counselors" Gene and Barbara, greeted us by scanning our eyeballs with their Apple Watches and then saying our names. I said, "You could have just asked, we speak English, you know," but they didn't hear because they were too busy looking at the screens of their iPads, iPhones and watches. They were very polite, but I got a weird vibe from them, and I remembered a word my English teacher had taught us recently: fore-shadowing. I had a feeling that this week was not going to go well.

Gene showed us to our tent, which was where we were going to sleep the first night. Each night we rotated with other campers to get the maximum "impact" from the "camp experience."

Brother, here we go!

Gene explained to us the swim challenge would begin at noon, and to be punctual or we'd be disqualified. And, if we were disqualified from one event, we couldn't win Camper of the Week. That person supposedly gets a big mystery prize. That's all I needed to hear! I thought it would be a week of swimming in ponds and staring at ducks, but a PRIZE is involved so I set my sights on winning. Not coming in second place, but winning!

Kenny and I arrived at the pool on time and had begun to stretch on the side when I noticed a group of boys around my age with shifty eyes hobble over to the pool together. They all plunged in at the same time and had that guilty look on their faces which got me suspicious. With my goggles on, I walked to the edge of the pool to see what they were up to, but didn't see anything so I forgot about them.

You know what? I learned that day that I am not a very fast swimmer despite the fact that while I was swimming I kept saying **'MICHAEL PHELPS, you're MICHAEL PHELPS'** over and over in my head. Didn't work. I got eliminated in the first round, but Kenny went a few more rounds (he's got a lot of nervous energy that really helps in these situations, I think) and I was in the bleachers cheering him on, looking through my nifty little pair of binoculars when I spotted a rat! (Not a real one. That would be gross!) No, this was a cheater!

Those four suspicious-looking kids kept beating everyone during every heat, and I got suspicious because who is that good all the time, right? Well, before one race I noticed one of them dove underwater, reached down for something at the bottom of the pool and attached it to his feet. It's a good thing my binoculars have a super intense zoom feature because I was able to see what he was attaching to his feet were transparent flippers. That's why he won, and that's why the other three kids in his little cheating posse won, too! No one else noticed except me, and I was fuming. I ran down to the edge of the pool to tell Kenny, but one of those crazy iPad people wouldn't let me get near the "active competitors." I squinted at the whole gang of them and gave them the evil eye, which is something my grandmother had taught me.

I stared all four of those cheating campers directly in the eyes, letting them know I was onto them, only, I'll admit, I was scared and was reluctant to tell on them because then who knows what they would do for revenge.

That day there were a couple other challenges: a Spelling Bee, and a Math Bee, which really were boring, and then a long assembly which made the Bees seem interesting. After dinner, we all gathered around a fire for story time, and what I thought would be making and eating S'mores, but instead, Gene and Barbara said S'mores weren't considered "healthful," (Ugh, that word!) and so we were going to make them with kale and quinoa (pronounced KEEN'wä), two things I had never heard of, let alone know what they were. They said they'd be called S'lesses. When I heard that I just lost it and screamed! **'KALE!!! QUINOA!!! Oh God, save me!!!'** And I threw myself dramatically on the floor which got a few laughs, but I think I freaked Gene and Barbara out because that wasn't written down on the agenda on their iDevices. "You should call them S'messes," I cried, still devastated.

Well, it turned out story time was a competition, too! It seemed to take forever and most of the stories were silly. When it was my turn, I told the story of the Angry Alligator and got a ton of laughs. Those conniving campers were fuming because they'd wanted to win that award, too. They each contributed a bit to a long story about an alien abduction that I could tell they worked hard on. But with stories, you know, there's that x-factor, and they didn't have it. So, ha! I won the badge, which apparently a college will care about when I'm asking for their permission for my parents to spend a lot of money for me to go there. After the campfire was extinguished, those creepy campers approached Kenny and me as we were heading to our tent.

"So you think you're all that for winning the story contest, huh?"

"I don't think it," I said, hoisting the certificate and the medal to show them proudly, "I KNOW it!" I was feeling good about myself because of my victory, but glancing over at Kenny who had run in the other direction, I could tell I may have gone too far.

"Yea, well, you'd better watch it. We're going to win the rest of the challenges, got it?"

I could see Gene and Barbara not far away so I felt bold at that moment: "You mean you're going to cheat like you did to win the swim competition today? Yea, I saw you down there with those invisible flippers. What if I told Gene and Barbara about your trick? Their iPads would NOT like that."

Then the smallest, slimiest looking one of the bunch, with a distracting mole on his cheek, approached me like a fearless little Yorkie.

"Well, you heard our story about the aliens, right?" he said.

"Yea," I said, nervously.

"Well, we've got a few aliens on our side, kid, and they won't like to hear that you're thinking of telling on us."

"Aliens! Ha. That's funnier than S'mores made with whatever it was," I said, turning my back on them and heading back to our tent.

Kenny and I were so darned tired after such a long day, and I was still thinking about those awful S'messes, that we both drifted off to sleep within minutes without saying a word.

I was sleeping soundly when I thought a dream was beginning, but I knew it was reality because I was sitting up and yawning and just then I saw it: A light shining on the side of my tent grew brighter and brighter, and I was paralyzed with fear. I couldn't even muster the strength to wake up Kenny. So, I don't even have a witness. Silhouetted in the light was the enormous, no, I mean, GIGANTIC bulbous head of an alien that was making a scary "Ooooh," sound.

"Ah, hello," I managed to say, petrified.

"I am an alien," the voice said, "just like the one in that story from tonight. Ooooh!"

"Christmas trees!" I cried (I learned that from my grandmother as a way to avoid saying something naughtier.)

"Yes, uh, Christmas trees," the alien replied. "Anyway, I have come from the sky in my spaceship to tell you to keep quiet and not tell on those other campers for cheating in the swim meet… Oooh! Because if you do, they, uh, we will take you back to a far-away planet where there's no AC and all they eat is kale and quinoa at every meal… Oooh!"

"Of course! I mean, no one cheated. We're all honest Abe's in here, right?"

"Right! Ooooh!"

Then the alien lifted its tiny arms like it was going to tackle the tent, and I ducked under the covers, trembling.

Kenny finally woke up all groggy and annoyed and pulled the covers off my head.

"Hey, Mikey, what's going on? I was sleeping."

"Kenny I just…I just…"

"You just what? Peed yourself? Woke up craving those kale and quinoa things? What?"

"I just saw an alien and it threatened to kidnap me!"

"Mikey, you know you are what people call CRAZY!"

"You call yourself my friend? You're supposed to believe me? This is INTENSE."

"And so is my desire to go back to sleep, Mikey. Good night!"

Can you believe him? I need to Google, "How to get a new best friend," right after I Google about that whole New and Old Mexico thing, but the camp confiscated all of our phones when we arrived and only Gene and Barbara have internet access. Ugh.

But first I have to get some sleep because tomorrow is another day jam-packed with challenges with those double-crossing campers!

Day 2

Breakfast the next morning was annoyingly healthy, but still kind of tasty: oatmeal with nuts and shriveled little red fruits, and some sort of fluffy egg white concoction on the side. But what was really odd was that even breakfast was a challenge. There were little slips of paper on everyone's tray, and we had to guess the nutritional information of each food item. The person who came the closest would win and get 10 points toward **"Camper of the Week."** As much as I wanted to win, I knew I'd lose this challenge because who cares about calories except for those Weight Watchers people? So, on the paper, I just drew a fully-decorated Christmas tree, which is surprisingly easy to do well.

At the end of the meal, Gene stood on a table, which I thought was unnecessary and a bit too dramatic and announced the winner of the breakfast challenge:

"Harriet Simpson!" he cried, and I thought I was hallucinating, but I pinched my arm and it hurt so I knew it was real.

"How did she get to New Mexico?" I asked Kenny.

"Probably in a plane, like us."

"I know that! But how did she know about this camp? I mean, what are the odds, right?"

Then Kenny turned red and had that guilty look people get.

"Spill it!" I said.

"Well, I knew she was coming, but I figured if I told you, you wouldn't want to come."

"You're right! Go with your instincts! Trust the force, Luke!"

Just then, Harriet walked over to our table, showing off her little blue ribbon like a proud pony. **"Hellllooooo!"** she said, hoisting the ribbon to my face.

"So you know how many calories are in oatmeal and nuts. Big deal, nutrition girl!"

"I'm 10 points closer to winning now!" She was beaming. What a nightmare.

"Doesn't matter. That little tribe of creeps from wherever is going to win," I said, pointing to them across the cafeteria.

"A group can't win unless they are all tied, and that is not likely to happen. It will probably be one person," Harriet said.

"Well, it's going to be one of them."

I could hear blips and bleeps and knew Gene and Barbara were approaching with their technology. Not looking us in the eye, glancing at their screens, they told us that there's an archery challenge, but before that, there's a Bee Bee.

"A Bee Bee?" I asked.

"Yes," Barbara replied, pressing buttons on her fancy watch. "It starts in 17 minutes and it's a challenge to see who knows the most about bees. It's kind of like a Spelling Bee, but about bees, get it?" Then she finally looked at me because she was pleased that she'd said something she thought was funny and was looking at me for confirmation the way people do.

"Yea, I get it. FUNNY!"

The Bee Bee was as exciting as you'd think it'd BE. I wish they hadn't taken all of our phones and iPads because sitting there in the audience would have been the perfect time to play silly phone games. Those cheating campers got close to winning the Bee Bee, but some goofy little kid from Hawaii who pronounced it, "Huh-WAH-ee," wound up winning, which was actually a big relief.

The archery challenge was INTENSE.

There were about a hundred targets and kids were shooting arrows like rain, only sideways and kind of scary and potentially dangerous, I thought. I really wanted to win this one, and thought I could because I had taken an archery class the previous summer and knew all the basics. I could feel my pulse quicken as I glanced over at those boys. I imagined that I was Robin Hood shooting arrows at, um, whatever he shot arrows at. I took my aim, made sure I was as still as could be, and then zoom, the arrow flew through space missing the target entirely. Darn it!

I got eliminated and then stood by on the side watching. Kenny got eliminated a little while after I did, and he stood beside me as we cheered on everyone that wasn't Harriet or those four cheaters. It turned out those creepy cheaters were really good at archery! I was standing there zoning out, staring out at the horizon, wondering why people say 'Bless you' when you sneeze, but not when you cough, when Kenny pulled at my sleeve.

He was FREAKING OUT!

"Mikey! Those kids are cheating. Look at them!"

I glanced over and saw two of them huddled behind a tree, attaching something to the tips of the arrows. What could it be? Kenny and I were standing there rubbing our chins, because that's what you do when you want to know something.

"Mikey, I think I figured it out. Look at the arrow just before it hits the target — it looks like it's going to miss but then it veers in the right direction. See that? Look!"

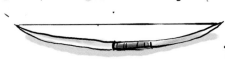

18

"Christmas Trees! You're right!"

"Christmas Trees?"

"Yea, it's something my grandma says. I kind of like it. She says that to avoid saying something naughty."

"Right. So they're putting magnets on the tips of the arrows. Those creeps!"

"We're gonna cook their goose!" I added.

"Ah, sure... ok."

That night, after dinner, it was story time, again, around the fire. The dessert was tolerable: berries and cream, so I didn't lose it and fall to the ground dramatically, which was good. Our challenge was to tell an interesting story, and I was determined to win again so I thought of something good while everyone else told their predictable, boring tales.

Finally it was my turn...

There was once a hive of bees in search of a queen who had decided it was too lonely at the top, so she demoted herself to be a worker bee and the transition was easy because bees look the same, even to other bees. She left her throne and crown for her replacement, but the bees couldn't decide who to promote because they had to admit they were all the same, and the proof of that was that none of them had a name. They decided to have challenges and games and crown the new queen or king based on who won the most points. The problem was that different bees won different contests: One won the honey eating contest; another won the honey bee; and yet another won the honey toss. They decided to break the tie by having two more competitions: a swim meet (in a pool of honey, of course) and an archery contest (instead of arrows, they'd shoot stingers, naturally), except a group of four shady-looking bees from the wrong side of the hive decided to cheat. Well, they won, and then the hive had a problem: they couldn't have four kings. So those four cheating campers, I mean, bees, chose the most crooked one to be the king, and because he didn't deserve the job, he ruined the hive, and a big bear sensed their weakness and took one swipe, and that was the end of them... all because of a band of cheating... bees.

After I finished my tale, I looked over at those cheating campers and they DID NOT look happy, but I didn't care. Kenny and I made our way back to our cottage which was where we were sleeping that night. It was far into the woods, but there was a path and a lantern here and there to guide the way. After I brushed my teeth and got into my PJ's, I decided we had to tell on those cheaters -- that if we didn't, then no one would.

"Kenny, it's time. We have to report those creeps to Gene and Barbara."

"Mikey, they are going to want revenge. I say we just keep quiet and forget about it. We're not going to win anyway."

"Speak for yourself! I've got 80 points already for winning the story contest two nights in a row. I'm getting close, you know."

"Ok, fine, but what good will come from telling on them?"

"It's just not right. From *The Angry Alligator* and *The Borrowed Bracelet*, I've learned a thing or two. What's right is right, and we have to tell them. Put on your Crocs and let's go."

"Now? Can't we just wait until the morning?"

"No! Justice cannot wait," I said, puffing out my chest like Superman.

It was late and, to be honest, it was kind of scary walking through the forest at night. Most of those lanterns had been turned off, so it was super dark, but we just followed the path, knowing it would lead to the little village of cabins where Gene and Barbara lived and charged their technology.

"Hooooooooo!" An owl that I didn't even know was there on a branch above us nearly scared the both of us to death.

"Mikey, I'm scared. Let's go back and tell them in the morning, like I said."

"No! We must prevail."

"Prevail?"

"Yes, it means to win. I heard it on TV, then looked it up on online, and now it's my new favorite word."

"I thought 'nugget' was your favorite word?"

"That was last month. Keep up."

Slowly, we were making our way through the winding trail down the hill, when we heard a branch snap behind us.

We froze.

"Ah hello... Are you out there?" I said.

Silence.

We were about to continue when, above our heads, we spotted a small flying object in the dark, hurtling towards us so we both screamed, "NO!" It landed a few feet from us and as we slowly approached it, we realized it appeared harmless, so we knelt down to examine it.

"It's a saucer for a tea cup," Kenny said, puzzled.

"Why would anyone throw a saucer in the air at us? I mean that's crazy." Then I thought about it a bit more and suddenly it made sense!

"Call the FBI! Call the CIA! Call Ellen! It's a flying saucer, get it? We're going to get kidnapped to a strange planet where they eat kale and quinoa all day and there's no AC! HELP!"

"Mikey, relax. The flying saucers you're talking about are totally different and much MUCH bigger."

"I know, but this was a sign, you know, FORESHADOWING, that the real one is coming, just wait. And, by the way, I didn't tell you this, but last night an alien visited our tent and told me not to say anything about those cheating campers."

Just then, the four cheating campers emerged from behind four trees, as if on cue. Their arms were crossed, and they did not appear pleased. Kenny and I were too scared to scream this time, so we just froze.

"Where are you two headed?" The biggest, scariest one of them who kind of looked like a bear (only much less hairy) said.

"Ah, we're going to... grandmother's house... and... yea... so that's why we're leaving bread crumbs... so we can find our way back."

"Mikey, that's Little Red Riding Hood and Hansel & Grettel combined," Kenny said. "That's not what we're doing!"

"You're supposed to be on my side! Just go with it!" I cried, glaring at Kenny.

"Listen, if you're thinking of reporting us to Gene and Barbara, we would like to give you forty reasons not to."

"Forty? There's a list?" I said.

Just then they all made fists, slowly, one finger at a time, all 40 of them, and gritted their teeth like mad dogs.

"Run!" Kenny screamed, and the two of us sprinted back to our little cottage and bolted the door. Panting, I told Kenny that now we couldn't tell on that band of bandits. We had no choice.

"Well, what are we going to do?"

"I don't know, but something will come to me... I know it will," I said, rubbing my chin.

Day 3

The next morning, I woke up before my alarm and just lay there for a while contemplating things. This is certainly an exciting week and many of the activities here are fun, but... it's just too much for me. Why can't adults realize all of these tests and competitions can really be very stressful for kids? As much as I want to win, what's wrong with sometimes just having some good old-fashioned fun for no prizes? I wonder if those cheating campers started their deception because all of the pressure just got too much for them? I mean, they weren't born cheaters, right? They chose cheating, and they can go back to being law-abiding citizens once again, I think.

I remember there were a couple of times in school when I kinda sorta cheated, but not really. In second grade, we had a spelling test and the words *skeptical* and *optimistic* were on it. I was able to spell them easily, but I just couldn't remember the meanings of them despite the fact that I studied my buns off. Henry Hamlin, who was seated next to me during the test, usually got good grades, so I decided to see how flexible my neck could be. I stretched and stretched and stretched, trying to see his paper until my teacher made a strange, suspicious face at me. Then, I just took the test on my own and – of course! – I mixed up the meanings of those words and got an 80 instead of a 100. And you know what? I didn't really mind that much because I was the one who earned that 80, not someone else. Sure, it would have felt great to get a 100, but it wouldn't have been a REAL 100 because it would be Henry's 100, you know what I mean?

Another time I was tempted to cheat, I wrote out on a tiny piece of paper the capitals of all of the states in the west that we were being tested on that day. I put the paper in the front pocket of my jeans. I was going to reach for the cheat sheet when the teacher had her back turned, but the mere thought of doing it and getting caught and humiliated in front of everyone was too stressful for me to handle. I even started hyperventilating, thinking about getting caught. Then my teacher

asked me if I was ok, if I wanted to go to the nurse.

In both of those instances I seriously contemplated doing the wrong thing, so I understand those other kids, but, really, they've gone overboard. I must find a way to stop them...

Just then, Kenny started singing in his sleep again. Every now and then he does it, and, to be honest, it's kind of entertaining, but a bit unsettling.

"Oh, I wish I was a little bar of soap," he sang. I chimed in with, *"Bar of soap!"* because I knew the song.

"Oh, I wish I was a little bar of soap."

"Bar of soap!"

"I'd go slippy, sloppy, slidy over everybody's heinie, Oh, I wish I was a little bar of soap."

Ok, Kenny wake up! We've got to eat before today's crazy challenges...

Today's big challenge was a REALLY eXtreme obstacle course called Obstacle Course!

There was swimming, biking, army crawling, tire jumping, rock climbing, pole vaulting, and SO much more it would take forever to list them all. I rolled up my sleeves and gritted my teeth at the thought of all of those challenges, and decided I was going to win Camper Of The Week by saying **COTW** over and over again like a battle cry.

We started after Gene and Barbara pressed a bunch of buttons on their devises and a giant red light turned yellow, then green. (Why couldn't they just say, 'Go?')

There were at least a hundred of us at the starting line. I adjusted my head band and wrist bands which kind of made me feel bizarre but seemed to suit the moment, and was off like lightning! I left Kenny in the dust as I ran like a greyhound an impressive distance, then swam a few laps before heading out into the forest to find my camper number pinned to a tree. It was a sort of scavenger hunt but less imaginative. Man, was it stressful to find my number among all of those other numbers tacked to trees but, as I neared the shore of a lake, I found mine. Near me was that skinny, goofy kid from Hawaii who had won the Bee Bee. He waved at me and was huffing and puffing, but eventually found his number and rejoined the race. I didn't bother to run because I knew I could catch up to him easily. He wasn't very fast, but he sure was steady, I'll give him that.

Just then I heard a voice.

"Hey kid, help us!" It was that creepy cohort of cheating campers and they were marooned on a little island in the middle of the lake. The boat they'd taken to get there had sprung a leak and was sinking fast. They were on the shore of that tiny island looking so helpless and desperate that I thought I may help them, but, checking first to see that no one was listening, I yelled out,

"Ha! You're stuck, aren't you?

Maybe it's karma for all of that cheating and threatening me. Think of THAT?"

"Listen, kid, we're sorry, just come out here in a boat and get us and we promise to stop."

"Are you just saying that because if I don't help, YOU not only will not win, but you'll spend all of your lives on that island? Or do you really mean it?"

"We mean it! Really we do."

They seemed sincere so I did it, I helped them. I paddled a boat out there and they got in, and then with all five of us paddling we got back to shore really quickly. I assumed we'd talk about the cheating and the flying saucer incident, but there was an odd silence in the boat among us.

They thanked me and, again, seemed sincere. But you never know, do you, when someone apologizes how sincere the apology is? You can't read people's minds. It's really very frustrating.

I tried my best to get back to the race after stopping in the forest for a few minutes to rest and drink water. But I couldn't really figure out which way to go. I started to get scared, and then I noticed a sort of trail in the distance over the hill so I went in that direction. The trail zig-zagged a bit, then there was a nifty little foot bridge that led over a stream which I crossed, and let's be honest, who doesn't love crossing a stream on a footbridge? I figured that the trail had to lead somewhere so I was no longer nervous, and I began to whistle and stare at the scenery. I noticed a duck and six little ducklings waddling behind, approaching the lake. Nature really is kind of beautiful and extraordinary when you stop for a moment and just take it in, isn't it?

Well, guess what? I just walked out of the forest, whistling and minding my business, when the trail I was on led straight to a sort of muddy pit that was clearly a part of the race. I paused for a moment, looked around, didn't see anyone so I just got into that mud pit and ran through it as fast as I could. The pit was long and turned a corner and then I could hear cheers and whistles and flags flying, and I thought maybe they were filming a movie, but they weren't. It was the finish line, and they were cheering me on. I knew there was a lot more of the race to finish because I hadn't completed at least two of the events that were listed on the race list so I was a bit confused. When I crossed the finish line a bunch of the adult camp employees and, of course, Gene and Barbara, were there to congratulate me and hoist

my muddy body above their heads, declaring me the winner!

I was stunned. I mean, I knew I had those other events to do, but I was tired and didn't realize I would win. And, besides, I didn't get lost in the forest intentionally. I just stumbled out of there near the end of the race and won. I knew I should have told Gene and Barbara that it was a mistake, that I hadn't really won, but it felt so good hearing all of those people cheer, and then I glanced down at my medal, and the applause was getting louder and louder, and it felt SO good that I didn't want it to end. I didn't want to give up the glory. I started to feel like the Grinch who stole Christmas, though, because inside my chest I thought I could feel my heart shrinking and shrinking as I stopped caring about winning honestly and now just wanted to WIN at all costs! My "victory" in the obstacle course earned me 100 points, putting me near the top of that society of swindlers.

COTW... COTW... COTW!

Still riding high, enjoying the praise, I screwed up my eyes and let out a nasty evil-person laugh,

HA HA HA! and started to think of ways to ensure that I would win Camper of the Week. After all, because I didn't admit that I hadn't completed all of the challenges, I am now a cheater, right? I felt deep down that I couldn't go back, that because I'd won this race dishonestly and decided not to say anything that I was now a new kind of person: I was a cheater — I'd crossed the line, and there was no going back. It felt pretty bad, but if this was my new identity, I thought I had to embrace it.

Tomorrow there would be more challenges and, while some were nearly impossible to cheat at, others, I'm sure, I could think of ways around. For example, there is a French competition after lunch and you're not supposed to enter it if you know any French already. It's really a memory test — there will be a teacher teaching a lesson and the camper that remembers the most will win another 20 points. The thing is, my uncle Anthony has been teaching me French for years. So I am sure to win that one, and by not telling them I already know some French, I am cheating, I admit it.

OUI OUI OUI,
bring it on!

Day 4

At breakfast the next morning, Harriet sat next to Kenny and me, and I was ok with that for some reason. Breakfast was a protein bar that was said to contain as much protein as an omelet and bacon. When I asked why we couldn't just have the omelet and bacon, I got one of those severe silent stares from the cafeteria lady that scared me for a moment.

"You know what," Harriet said, bunching up the wrapper of the protein bar, "I think those kids over there are cheating."

My heart began to race. Did she know about me, too?

"Ah, why do you say that, Harriet?" I asked nervously.

"I don't know. It's kind of fishy how they are winning so many competitions. I'm determined to catch them, and when I do, I will tell on them and they will get disqualified and kicked out of camp and banned for life from all competitions in this world!"

Oh no! That'll happen to me, too! I was so nervous I didn't know what to do so I changed the subject.

"So, ah, do you guys believe in aliens?"

"No. They don't exist, except that lonely people in the countryside sometimes think they see flying saucers, only no one's ever around to witness it, and they're really just hungry and far from the fridge so they hallucinate. That's my theory," Harriet said.

"I agree!" said Kenny. "We'd better go. The French competition starts in a few minutes."

Then we made our way to the classroom and, as I'd expected, I won because I already knew those words, and the victory didn't even feel good because I knew I was cheating. Ugh. I wish I could stop, but it feels like I'm stuck in a hamster wheel of cheating and can't get off. What should I do?

Next there was an arts and crafts contest, and by this point I was so exhausted I just wanted to go home. But I had two more days of this craziness to endure before that.

The arts and crafts competition was kind of weird because there would be judges and they would decide which entry was the best. I thought that was odd, but got an idea. My mother had put the necklace she'd made when she was in camp years ago in my suitcase for good luck. It's really nice and ornate and not something I could ever do. I sat next to Kenny trying to replicate it and what turned out was a disaster. I really am not good at arts and crafts it turns out. I looked over at Kenny and he was busying himself making a mini totem pole of the cast of Full House, only they looked like monkeys, not people. He looked happy with his creation so I didn't want to burst his little bubble. I just sat there disappointed in myself for not being able to make anything good and wondered if anyone would discover I'd cheated at the obstacle course and the French contest. Then I got an idea.

I excused myself and said I had to go back to my cabin to do something "personal." Gene and Barbara didn't dare question me because I think they thought it had to do with toilet activity. I walked back to my cabin, but on my way there, I felt like someone was following me. Every now and then I'd hear a twig snapping, but when I'd turn around, there was no one there.

I rummaged through my suitcase and found the necklace my mother made when she was in camp and put it in my pocket. I returned to my bench in the arts and crafts building and pretended to be working on my masterpiece. When time was called, I reached into my pocket and took out my mother's exquisite necklace and submitted it for judging.

"Wow, you made that necklace really fast!" Kenny said.

"Well, yea, I guess…" I said.

"What do you mean, you guess? It didn't just appear, so you made it. Be proud!"

"Kenny, there's something I have to tell you."

"Oh no, Mikey, what is it? What are you up to now?"

Before I could say a word, I heard my name being called by the judges. My necklace (or, my mother's) had won!

I approached the podium, trembling and convinced that I was going to be outed as a cheat in front of everyone, but that didn't happen. I won 25 points toward Camper of the Week and was now in first place. Glancing at the crowd, I spotted that scary band of brats who were scowling at me. After the event ended, they approached me. The one that looked like a bear started...

"Kid, we know you cheated and we have proof."

"How can you have proof? And, ah, I didn't cheat. That's a foul accusation!"

"Oh, yea? Here's the proof." Then his friend who reminded me of a pelican because he had a tiny body and a big head and nose, took out his iPhone.

"Hey, you're not supposed to have your phone this week!" I said, upset at this infraction.

"Well, I managed to smuggle mine in. Take a look at this..."

Then he handed me the phone and played the video of me walking back to my cabin and taking my mother's beautiful necklace back to the arts and crafts competition and submitting it as my own.

"That's it. My goose is cooked," I said, devastated.

"Not yet," one of the other cheaters said. He looked like a bug because he had big eyes and even bigger glasses. "If you throw the rest of the challenges, we'll erase the video."

"Throw the challenges? How can I throw a challenge? I'm not that strong. Look at these arms," I said, making a muscle which you couldn't even see because it was so tiny.

"'Throwing the challenges means you need to lose the rest of the challenges on purpose. You have to deliberately do terribly."

Oh, dang! Now they had me. I had to agree or they would release that video and it would go viral and my life would be ruined. People all over the world would see me in the act of cheating! What would Ellen think? I couldn't disappoint her.

So I agreed.

That afternoon there was a pole vaulting challenge, and I only vaulted a few inches before falling to the ground intentionally. Then there was a rock climbing challenge that I got disqualified from because I attempted to do it backwards, climbing the air. I quickly fell from first to third and then sixth place behind that weird kid from Hawaii who turned out to be quite nice, in fact.

He just kept plugging away at everything, doing his best, and never complaining. He never won a thing, but pretty consistently came in fifth or sixth place, and he didn't seem to mind. In fact, he seemed to genuinely enjoy the challenges, and I wished I could be more like him.

That night I couldn't sleep a wink. I was tormented by the thought of that video of me cheating going viral. I imagined it playing on every phone and computer in the world. People in China, India, and even astronauts would gasp in horror when they saw how despicable I was.

I needed fresh air, so in my PJ's I walked into the forest. Then, in a clearing, I dropped to my knees. I was in agony, like Jesus in the desert (I learned about that in religion recently), and began to pray for salvation, hoping I wouldn't be tempted to cheat again.

"Lord, give me the STRENGTH!"

I cried, but then I remembered the mother duck (or it could have been a father, let's face it, it's hard to tell) with six little duckling children by the lake the other day. It was a sign! From now on I would fall

into place and follow along, just like those little ducklings. Every time I go astray, I mess up. If one of the little duckies did that he would probably starve because he needs the others to survive. Yes! That's it. I am happiest when I do what is right, and miserable when I do what is wrong. I pretty much always know the difference deep down every time.

Smiling with my new wisdom, I headed back to my cabin, but it occurred to me that I'd have to first apologize for my cheating. Yes, I would do that the next day, right after breakfast… or maybe lunch… or dinner… or, no, maybe I'd wait till just before I was about to leave. No, I've got it! I'd write an apology poem to the camp like I did to the alligator a couple of months ago and it would all be over. Only that felt wrong. It felt cowardly to wait so long. Ugh. Why does life get so complicated when I do these things? Why can't I be like that Hawaiian kid and just be happy with what I have and not hatch these crazy schemes?

Tomorrow, I decided, getting into bed, I'd apologize for cheating… Or, at least, I'd try.

Day 5

The next morning at breakfast I sat next to that Hawaiian boy because I could see he was alone. Kenny and Harriet were talking to some annoying kids about becoming famous Instagrammers or something and so I figured this kid couldn't be worse.

His name was Kai which means he had to say, "Hi, my name is Kai."

"That rhymes," I said, pleased.

He smiled because he'd probably heard that before, but didn't want to tell me that. I told him my name.

"Is everything ok?" he asked, "because you were in first place, now you're all the way down to fifth."

"Nah, I'm fine. I'm just losing the desire to compete, you know. It's really about the journey. I didn't even realize this camp was so intense until I got here. I mean, wow, right? Did you realize it?"

"Yea, but it doesn't really matter to me. I came here because it had such a wide variety of events, and I find that fun. Every other camp is just arts and crafts, or sports or something, but not all of this. I find it exciting."

"You don't find all of these challenges stress-ful?"

"No, not really. I just focus on the challenge and don't think about the outcome."

"That's great, Kai, I wish everyone else could see it that way. Wait, I just said Kai, I — that rhymes."

"I know my father used to say that and smile whenever he'd say my name and then I."

"Used to?

"Yes, well, it's kind of personal, and I'm not really in the mood to talk about it, if that's ok?"

"Sure, I'm sorry, Kai."

"No problem."

I spent the next half hour talking to him about video games, Encyclopedia Brown books, building forts, and Japanese pencil cases. It was a fun conversation.

After I said good bye to Kai (I had to say, "Good bye, Kai!" which pleased me again because it rhymed), I headed over to the main building to find the camp masters so I could apologize for cheating. I opened the door to the auditorium, and it appeared that a dance challenge had just ended and the judges were still at a table on the stage. I approached them.

"Ah, hi, my name is Michael McMichaels, and I have, ah, something to share with you." I had thought apologizing would be easier, but I was shaking.

"Ok, sure, what is it?" The man at the end of the judges' table said. He was the oldest looking of the bunch, and I think he was probably the head of the whole camp.

"Well, you see, it's um, difficult... to... um... say..." I thought I was going to pee myself. My heart was racing, my cheeks were on fire, and I was sweating like, well, like someone who has cheated and doesn't know how to stop, or how to admit it.

"Michael, is everything ok?" the man asked. "What do you have to share with us?"

"Ah, yea, well, I just wanted to..."

I simply couldn't do it. I could not confess that I had cheated, but there they were all lined up behind that table in front of me, and they'd probably send me to the camp psychologist if I didn't say or do something.

An idea came to me!

"I've been working on a little number, want to see it?"

"Sure!" the camp master said.

"Do you have music?" I asked. "Beyoncé?"

"You bet. Here you go!"

When the music filled my ears, I did it. I began to dance like a mad man. I leapt, I flung my body all over, I twirled, I pirouetted, I did other things that probably don't have fancy names because no one has ever done them before — and there's probably a reason for that. I huffed and I puffed, and still that music was playing so I kept dancing, dancing, dancing. It was a thing of beauty. I was poetry in motion.

When the song finally ended, I was on the floor doing a kind of crab walk. The judges were so impressed that they just sat there in silence for a while. **Maybe they'd call *America's Got Talent* to get me an audition? Maybe they'd offer to send me to New York to go to ballet school or something for free?**

"Michael, ah, that was, ah, extraordinary, to say the least," the camp master said, shocked.

"Thank you!"

"Yes, please return to where you should be now. I'm sure someone is expecting you to be somewhere. And, again, that was a truly, ah, extraordinary display, truly extraordinary."

"Thank you, sir!"

On my way out of the main building I glanced into the library across the hall and saw Kenny and Harriet reading books and then scribbling things down on small pieces of paper so I decided to approach them.

"Hey guys, what are you doing?"

"Doing? Ah, we're reading..." Kenny said, flustered.

"What's to be embarrassed about? Reading is fundamental, you know."

"We're done though, right Kenny?" Harriet said, slamming her book closed. "Ok, guys let's get going. We're going to be late to the poetry contest if we don't hurry."

Then we ran to the cottage by the lake where

the poetry contest was being held, I guess because that was a poetic location. A bunch of kids read poems about birds, horses, and princesses, and I was really bored. I had no intention of entering that one (because I am poetry – I don't write it) and was surprised when I saw Kenny write his name down to enter.

I was just sitting there bored out of my mind when I glanced over at Harriet and Kenny who were sitting next to each other. Very discreetly, they both took out the little pieces of paper that they'd stuck in their pockets in the library and read them until their names were called. They were about to read the poems they'd copied from library books! Oh no! Now Kenny and Harriet are cheaters, too. What's the world coming to?

Oh, yea. I've been cheating too. Kind of forgot that for a moment.

Kenny was first. He approached the mic.

"This poem is called 'To Thomas Butts'." Everyone in the room giggled.

"To my friend Butts, I write
My first vision of light,

On the yellow sands sitting.
The sun was emitting his glorious beams.
From heaven's high streams."

"And that's my poem," he said and everyone clapped. He took his seat next to me.

"Pretty good, huh?" Kenny said, smiling.

"Pretty good, my chin!" I said. "You copied that from the library book. You're nothing but a cheater, cheater, gas-meter reader!"

"Gas meter reader? Where in the world did that come from? Isn't it supposed to be pumpkin eater?"

"Me! It's original. I came up with it because I'm CREATIVE!

Do you know the kind of trouble you can get in for cheating? You are INCREDIBLE!" I said, conveniently forgetting for a moment about what I, myself, had done.

Then Harriet approached the mic.

"My poem is called 'Ode to Duty,'" she said in her annoyingly perfect English accent, and everyone giggled again.

"Stern Daughter of the Voice of God!

O Duty! If that name thou love
Who art a light to guide, a rod
To check the erring, and reprove;
Thou, who art victory and law
When empty terrors overawe;
From vain temptations dost set free;
And clam'st the weary strife of frail
    humanity!"

Everyone clapped and Harriet took her seat. She was glowing, but it wouldn't last for long because Gene stepped up to the mic with all of his technology and asked Harriet and Kenny to approach him.

The room fell silent.

"Is there something you two would like to share with us?" Gene asked.

Both Harriet and Kenny said, no, there wasn't.

"Well, according to my devices, BOTH of those poems are not original. They are classics of English literature by Blake and Wordsworth. You plagiarized their work!"

Just then, Kenny and Harriet bowed their heads in shame and everyone in the audience started to boo loudly, except, of course, for me. I wanted to boo for just Harriet, but that wasn't possible, so I just sat there and watched as Gene took each of them by the wrist and escorted them off stage.

"Where do you think he's taking them?" I asked the kid seated next to me.

"He's taking them to the lion cage to be eaten."

"WHAT?"

"Just kidding! He's probably going to call their parents and disqualify them from being Camper of the Week."

I can't believe it! My best friend got humiliated in front of the whole camp, and I just sat there and did nothing. But he did cheat, right? I mean, I'm guilty of the same crime only I haven't gotten caught… yet. What if those creepy cheaters show their video of me cheating to the rest of the campers? This is really a big mess. I have no idea what to do. I am trying to be a little obedient duckling, waddling behind the others, and it's not working. I'm tormented by guilt, but I don't want those creeps to win. I have to confront them tonight and tell them that I have to turn us all in, that it's the right thing to do.

After lights out, I made my way over to their tent and thought about knocking, but then I realized that you can't knock on a tent, so I just sort of leaned in and said, "Hey, guys, you in there?"

They all went silent and then the zipper slowly lowered and all four of them stuck their heads out, one on top of the other like a totem pole of angry kids.

"Wow, how did you do that?" I asked.

"Never mind. What do you want, kid?"

"I just wanted to let you guys know that I think we have to turn ourselves in for cheating and apologize to everyone. It's the

64

right thing to do. It's called a *moral imperative*."

"A what?" the one that looked like a bear asked.

"A moral imperative. It's an ethical responsibility to do the right thing. I learned about it in religion class, which, I'll admit, is often very boring, but every now and then they say something interesting like 'moral imperative.' You just have to listen and you'd be surprised what you will learn." Just then all four of them grabbed an arm or a leg of mine and squeezed really hard.

"Listen, religion nerd. We don't care about floral pedestrians or whatever you just said. We care about winning and we're currently ranked 1,2,3 and 4. If you tell on us and we get disqualified, we will have that alien take you to his planet, and it will not be pretty."

Oh no!
Kale, quinoa, and no AC!"

I screamed, slithering out from their slimy grips and running back to my dorm.

What a mess! Now what do I do?

Day 6

That night I thought I would never fall asleep, but, as usual, finally I did, and I had the worst dream. I was on one of those TV courtroom shows that grown-ups love so much. I was being cross-examined by an alien in a very nice suit, and when I turned to face the judge, it was the cheater who looked like a bug. What's worse, the jury box was filled with people eating kale chips and cooling themselves with hand-held fans. They must be from that planet where the alien will take me to. I started crying out in my sleep: **"No kale chips, please, no! Someone turn on the AC! I am GUILTY! GUILTY! GUILTY!"**

Then I felt Kenny shake me. I didn't even see him in the bed next to mine the night before when I'd gone to sleep, that's how scared and tired I was.

"Mikey, wake up, you're dreaming."

"Kenny, it was a nightmare, really, you don't understand. They were all eating kale chips and there was no AC."

"I like kale!"

"Really?" You learn things about your friends all the time – it never ends.

Well, we have to get ready for breakfast. It's our last day, finally, and I just want to get home already.

"What did they do to you for cheating?"

"They gave us a really long lecture about how bad it is to cheat, and then they called our parents. My father got really mad at me and said I'd be punished when I got home."

"Why did you do it?" I asked, again, temporarily forgetting that I, too, had cheated, not once, not twice, but THREE times.

"I hadn't won a single competition, Mikey, and at first it didn't bother me, but seeing my name so far down on the leaderboard started to get to me. I mean, I'm not even a competitive kid. I just started to feel so down about myself that I thought the only solution was to cheat. You know what I mean?"

"Yes, I get it. What's going on in this world anyway that everything has to be so darn competitive? Remember in pre-K when we had fun learning before they started all of those crazy tests in kindergarten. **The adults are taking the joy out of EVERYTHING!** I think our grandparents should punish them for being out of line. That's the problem with adults – when they're wrong, who is there to point it out to them?"

"That's a good point. I think next year if my parents are willing to send me to a camp, I'm going to ask for a normal one where you can cook actual S'mores and just have fun. This place is too stressful."

"Kenny, I have something to tell you."

"Really, what?"

Then I told him about the cheating I'd done and not having the courage to admit it, and he understood. It really was a relief to get all of that off my chest. I also mentioned that those crooked creeps were going to send me to a strange planet where all they do is eat kale and quinoa and there's no AC. He laughed and said that's crazy, but I wasn't so sure.

"Come on, Mikey, let's get to breakfast. I'm really hungry."

After breakfast was the final challenge. It was an obstacle course that made the one from the other day seem like walking down the hallway in your house. The winner of this one would get 120 points and then there would be a ceremony for Camper of the Week.

Kenny and I got to the starting line, read the list of challenges that took up nearly a whole page, looked at each other and sighed.

"This is out of control, Kenny."

"I know, but what can we do?"

"I don't know, but I'm sure an idea will come to me…"

"Oh no, Mikey! When you get ideas, I get stressed. Let's just do this final event, pack up and go home, ok?"

"No!" I said confidently. "We must speak out.
I know what to do."

"Good grief," Kenny said.

I saw a megaphone on the stage that the
announcer would use to begin the obstacle course
so I made my way up there, whistling
like I was doing nothing out of the
ordinary. When no one was looking, I grabbed the megaphone,
lifted it to my lips and began:

"Attention campers!

Attention Campers!"

Everyone looked up at me, and for a moment I felt famous, but also nervous.

"Who here is fed up with all of this crazy competition? Who thinks that this week should really just be an opportunity to have some fun, meet some new people and eat actual S'mores and not some weird replacement that tastes terrible?"

A bunch of hands went up, but I could tell that some people were scared to be honest, thinking that they'd get disqualified, so I continued:

"All of this competition has led to rampant cheating. I am going to be honest with you all right now." I paused for a moment to gather the courage. "I cheated three times this week. I'm not proud of it, but the pressure got to me. And, as many of you know, Harriet and Kenny have also cheated. Who else has cheated because they felt overwhelmed by the pressure to win challenge after challenge? Come on, be honest now."

At first a few hands went up, then a few more, then many more and soon every single kid's hand went up. Except Kai's. He was just sort of standing there amazed, glancing around at everyone.

Then the camp master, who'd watched my dance routine approached me and asked for the megaphone. I thought he would yell at me, but he didn't.

"Attention campers," he said, "My name is Mr. Arnold and as many of you know I am the camp master. I truly had no idea there was such rampant cheating going on, and from what I hear, there were probably too many competitions this week and the pressure got to you. Am I right?"

Everyone nodded and said yes.

"Well, then, I am going to make some serious changes to this camp in the future, but that will take some time and planning. In the meantime, we should still crown a Camper of the Week, and based on what I've just seen, I think it should be Kai. Does everyone agree?"

Everyone nodded and said yes.

"Kai, please approach the stage."

Kai made his way through the crowd and approached Mr. Arnold.

"It is with great pleasure and pride that I declare you Camper of the Week for your integrity and grace under pressure." Everyone clapped and Mr. Arnold placed the medal over his head and handed him an envelope which he opened.

"Speech, speech!" I cried.

Kai accepted the megaphone timidly, but his voice was confident and clear.

"Campers, thank you for this award. I am truly humbled. I came here to honor my father who recently died of cancer. I miss him a lot, but one of the reasons I'm doing this is for him. He told me that life is more interesting when you get involved in things and don't just sit around waiting for stuff to happen. That's why I don't care if I win or not. I'm just getting involved. He told me to try my hardest, be honest, have integrity, but to also have fun. I am going to donate this hundred-dollar prize to cancer research." Everyone clapped. "And I have an idea. How about we all just enjoy ourselves for the rest of the day? No more competitions, no more winners and losers, just fun! Who agrees?"

Everyone cried out, "I do!" and "me!"

Mr. Arnold took the megaphone from Kai and thanked him.

"And so it will be. I officially declare that the challenges have ended, and the rest of the day is free for all of you to enjoy yourselves doing whatever you want. As Kai said, there will be no winners and no losers, so just enjoy!"

Everyone cheered and then scattered like squirrels. Some kids started to swim, others to make arts and crafts, and others actually wrote poetry because they liked doing that, not because they'd win a prize for it.

Mr. Arnold approached me.

"Michael, thank you. I wasn't aware of the pressure you campers were feeling. It would have been better if you had told me privately, but given the circumstances, I understand."

"Thank you, Mr. Arnold. And I want to apologize for cheating. I don't normally do that, but, like I said, the pressure got to me."

"Looks like you weren't alone. I hope you come back next year. There might be a challenge or two, but not nearly as many and there will be more fun, I promise."

"Sounds great, thanks!"

We shook hands, and I ran like lightening to the pool because I love to swim so much that I

think I'm actually part fish. As I was about to dive in, I felt a tap on my shoulder.

It was the band of cheating campers. My heart started to race. I was sure they wanted to beat me up for exposing all of the cheating and they probably weren't happy that Kai had won, so I quickly dove into the pool and swam to the other side. All four of them dove in after me and quickly caught up. My back was to the wall of the pool, and I was treading water. They got closer and closer. I tried to scream, but couldn't because I was so nervous. And, besides, there were no adults around to help me. **In fact, that area of the pool was empty except for me and now THEM. Oh no!**

"Please don't beat me up or send me to that kale, quinoa, and no-AC planet, please! I have a very bright future ahead of me."

The one that looked like a bear spoke for all of them.

"Look, kid, we're not going to beat you up, and we're not going to have that alien kidnap you because A) we were getting stressed, too, about getting caught, and we're relieved it's all over and B) there never was an alien — we made it up to scare you, but you knew that, right?"

"Ah, yea, of course I did," I said, embarrassed. "Everyone knows aliens don't exist. I mean, it's obvious, sure."

"Good. It would have been weird if you actually believed that there were aliens on the earth kidnapping kids. I mean, that's crazy."

"Totally. Listen, have a safe trip back home, ok? I'm going to find my friend Kenny now."

"Later."

"Later."

On the flight back home, Kenny won the coin toss for the window seat, and that kind of annoyed me because I like to look out at the clouds and down at the Earth getting smaller and smaller as we climb higher and higher. At any rate, he won fair and square.

"So that was a crazy week, huh?" Kenny said, flipping through the pages of one of those strange in-flight catalogs. Does anyone ever order these things?

"Yea," I said. "I'm glad we finally got to have some fun at the end there."

"Well, it's a good thing you grabbed hold of that megaphone and made that speech."

"Thanks. Took a lot of nerve, but I'm glad I did it."

Then, from the seat in front of us, we could see a bulb-headed alien slowly rising and rising

before us, its tiny green arms dangling as it said,

"Ooooh!"

Kenny and I looked at each other and were about to scream when we heard the alien giggle and snort, and I thought, Hey, I know that annoying laugh, but whose could it be?

Then the very angry flight attendant pulled at the top of the alien's head, removing the mask, and there was Harriet laughing her annoying laugh, her hair all messed up from the mask she'd made.

"Ha!" she said, still cracking up, "Gotcha!"

And I had to admit, she did.

Tips & Questions

"All of this competition has led to rampant cheating. I am going to be honest with you all right now."

I paused for a moment to gather the courage. "I cheated three times this week. I'm not proud of it, but the pressure got to me. And, as many of you know, Harriet and Kenny have also cheated. Who else has cheated because they felt overwhelmed by the pressure to win challenge after challenge? Come on, be honest now."

Here are some helpful tips and discussion questions to share with children:

1. **ASK** – Why is cheating wrong? How can it harm others and the cheater, as well?

2. **ASK** – Is cheating confined to the classroom? What are other ways people can cheat that aren't school-related? How are these other ways of cheating also harmful?

3. **DISCUSS** – In *The Creepy Campers*, it turned out that all but one camper was cheating. Is cheating wrong if everyone or nearly everyone is doing it? Why?

4. **SHARE** – Think of an instance in your life when you cheated. Why did you do it? How did you feel when you were doing it? If you were nervous, do you think that was a clue that the behavior was wrong? What did you gain from cheating? Who or what may have been harmed in the process? If you could go back in time, would you still have cheated?

5. **DISCUSS** – Why is it important to work hard and not be overly focused on the outcome?

6. **DISCUSS** – If you study for a test and get a bad grade, does that mean…

- …there is something wrong with you or that maybe the test was too difficult?

- …you could have studied even harder?

- …maybe your talents lie elsewhere, but you should still continue working as hard as you can?

7. **SHARE** – Have you ever witnessed someone cheating – maybe a friend – but lacked the courage to say something for fear of being called a "tattle tale" or for losing your friend?

8. **ASK/SHARE** – What is the value of honesty? Ask your child to give a concrete example of how being honest helped someone.

9. **ASK/DISCUSS** – What is your definition of success? Ask your child to define it for him/herself. Pin your child's definition up in a prominent place such as on the refrigerator, and insist that definition is the true meaning of the word, that we all get to define success for ourselves and amend the definition over time as we mature.

10. **ASK** – What is the true value of learning? How is it measured other than grades and report cards?

11. **DISCUSS** – Some kids feel there are valid excuses for cheating. Discuss each quote below with your child and reinforce why they are not valid reasons for cheating.

- "I don't like my teacher."

- "This subject isn't very important anyway."

- "I don't have time to study."

- "My parents expect me to get good grades."

12. **CONSIDER** – Parents and teachers, what can you do to lessen the pressure on children and let them know that their hard work, diligence, and honesty are more important than a high grade or a trophy earned by cheating?

Boys Town Press Featured Titles

Kid-friendly books to teach social skills

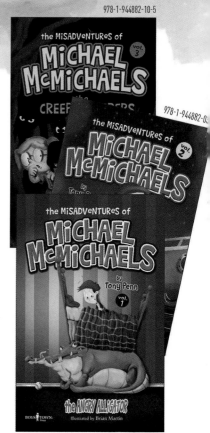

978-1-944882-10-5

978-1-944882-03...

978-1-934490-94-5

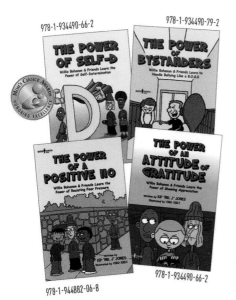

978-1-934490-66-2

978-1-934490-79-2

978-1-944882-06-8

978-1-934490-66-2

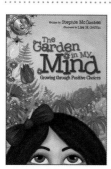

978-1-934490-54-9

978-1-934490-60-0

978-1-934490-87-7

978-1-934490-77-8

BoysTownPress.org

For information on Boys Town, its Education Model®, Common Sense Parenting®; and training programs:
boystowntraining.org, boystown.org/parenting
EMAIL: training@BoysTown.org, PHONE: 1-800-545-5771

For parenting and educational books and other resources:
BoysTownPress.org, EMAIL: btpress@BoysTown.org, PHONE: 1-800-282-6657